THE LIFE OF
TURPIN

RYLE & Co., Printers, 2 & 3, Monmouth-court, Bloomsbury

THE LIFE AND ADVENTURES
OF
RICHARD TURPIN,
A MOST
NOTORIOUS HIGHWAYMAN,
COMPRISING

A Particular account of all his Robberies, His Ride to York, and his Trial and Execution for Horse-stealing, April 7th, 1739.

Turpin Putting the old Woman on the Fire, to make her Confess where She had hid her Money.

RICHARD TURPIN was born at Hampstead, in Essex, where his father kept the sign of the Bell; and after being the usual time at school, he was bound apprentice to a butcher in Whitechapel, but did not serve out his time, for his master discharged him for impropriety of conduct, which was not in the least diminished by his parents' indulgence in supplying him with money, which enabled him to cut a figure round the town among the blades of the road and the turf, whose company he usually kept.

His friends, thinking that marriage would reclaim him, persuaded him to marry, which he did with one Hester Palmer, of East-Ham, in Essex, but he had not long been married before he became acquainted with a gang of thieves whose depredations terrified the whole county of Essex, and the neighbourhood of London. He joined sheep-stealing to foot-pad robbery; and was at last obliged to fly from his place of residence for stealing a young heifer, which he killed, and cut up for sale.

Soon after, he stole two oxen from one Farmer Giles, of Plaistow, and drove them to a butcher's slaughtering-house, near Waltham Abbey.

He was followed there, but made his escape out of the window of the house where he was, just as they were entering the door.

He now retreated into the Hundreds of Essex, where he found greater security: he adopted a new scheme; and that was to rob the smugglers, but he took care not to attack a gang, only solitary travellers, this he did with a colour of justice, for he pretended to have a deputation from the Customs, and demanded their property in the king's name.

He again joined the gang with whom he had before connected himself, the principal part of whose depradations were committed upon Epping Forest, &c.

But this soon becoming an object of magisterial enquiry, he again returned to the solitude of the country, with some more of the gang, and they became notorious deer-stealers, and Turpin being a good shot, sent many a buck up to his connections in London.

They next determined to commence house-breakers; and in this they were much encouraged by joining with Gregory's gang, as it was then called, a company of desparadoes that made he Essex and adjacent roads very dangerous to travel.

They robbed the house of Mr. Strype, an old man, who kept a chandler's shop at Watford, where they got a good booty.

In one night this gang robbed Chingford and Barking churches of all the moveables left in the vestries, but the plate of both places being placed in the respective churchwardens' possession, they got but an indifferent booty. Turpin eluded, with some of his companions, the search that was made after them; but three were taken, one of whom turning evidence, the other two were transported

Two months after this, he had the audacity to venture as far as Suson, in Essex, whither his wife had retired, and here he lived unnoticed six months; but being discovered, he made a quiet retreat, and nothing more was heard of him till the robbery of

Farmer Lawrence, when he joined with others, called the Essex gang, the principal of whom were Ned Rust, George Gregory, Fielder, Rose, and Wheeler.

Somehow or other, Turpin became acquainted with the circumstances of an old woman, that lived at Laughton, that kept a great quantity of cash by her; whereupon they agreed to rob her; and when they came to the door, Wheeler knocked and Turpin and the rest forcing their way into the house, blind-folded the eyes of the old woman and her maid, and tied the legs of her son to the bedstead, but not finding the wished-for boots, they held a consultation, as they were certain she must have e considerable sum concealed. Turpin told her that he knew she had money, and it was in vain to deny it, for have it they would. The old lady persisted she had none, but Turpin insisting she had money, he swore he would put her on the fire. She continued obstinate and endured for some time, when they took her off the grate, and robbed her of all they could find, upwards of four hundred pounds.

Early in 1730, they robbed a farmer near Barking, where the people not coming to the door soon, they broke it open. They then gagged, tied, and blind-folded all they could find in the place, and robbed the house of about 700l., which pleased Turpin so much, that he exclaimed, " Aye, this is the thing, that's your sort for the rag, if it would but last !" And they safely retired with their prize. The keeper of Epping Forest was fixed upon to feel the effects of their resentment for his vigilance in disturbing their poaching. But Turpin was not concerned in this affair, for, being in London, he forgot his appointment

Turpin's absence was a very unfortunate circumstance to the keeper's family, for they proceeded to greater lengths in their mischief than he would have permitted, as he was always satisfied with the plunder, without cruelty. In the general wreck, a China punch-bowl was broke, and out of it dropped 122 guineas, which they picked up and retired with.

They then took the road to London, and coming through Whitechapel, they met Turpin, with whom they went to the Bun-house, in the Rope-fields, where they shared their booty with him, which proves the old adage, " There is honour among thieves."

Their next robbery of note was about seven or eight o'clock n the evening. Rust, Turpin, Fielder, Walker, and three others came to the house of Mr. Saunders, a wealthy farmer, in Kent, and knocking at the door, which being opened, they all rushed in, went to the parlour, where Mr. Saunders, his wife, and some

Turpin meeting with King.

friends, were at cards; but desired them not to be frightened. The first thing they laid hands on was a silver snuff-box, and then secured the company, obliged Mr. Saunders to open his closets, boxes, &c from whence they took upwards of 100*l*., and all the plate in the house, finding some wine and eatables they enjoyed themselves, and got away safely.

They next proceeded into Surry, where Turpin and his company robbed Mr. Sheldon's house, near Croydon Church, where they arrived about seven o'clock in the evening. They secured the coach-man in the stable. His master hearing some strange voices in the yard, was proceeding to know the cause, when he was met by Turpin, who seizing hold of him, compelled him to show them the way into the house, when he secured the door, and confined the rest of the family in one room, here they found but little plate, and no cash. From Mr. Sheldon's person they took eleven guineas, two of which Turpin returned him, begged pardon for what they had done, and wished him a good night.

These robberies had hitherto been carried on entirely on foot, with only the occasional assistance of a hackney coach, but now they aspired to appear on horse-back, for which purpose they now hired horses at the Old Leaping Bar in Holborn, from whence they set out about two o'clock in the afternoon, and arrived at the Queen's Head, Stanmore, where they staid to regale themselves. It was by this means that Wood, the master of the house, had so good an opportunity of observing the horses, as to remember the same again when he saw them afterwards in Bloomsbury, where they were taken. About five they went from Mr Wood's to Stanmore and staid from six until seven and then went together for Mr. Lawrence's, about a mile from thence, where they got about half-past seven. On their arrival at Mr. Lawrence's, they alighted from their horses at the gate; whereupon Fielder knocked at the door, and calling out Mr. Lawrence. The man-servant thinking it to be some of the neighbours, opened the door, upon which they all rushed in with pistols, and seizing Mr. Lawrence and his man, threw a cloth over their faces, they then fell to rifling his pockets, out of which they took one guinea, and about fifteen shillings in silver, with his keys. They said that they must have more, and drove Mr. Lawrence up stairs, where, coming to a closet, they broke open the door, and took out from thence two guineas, ten shillings, a silver cup, 13 silverspoons, and two gold rings. They then rifled the house of all they could get, linen, table-cloths, shirts, and the sheets from off the beds; and trod the beds under feet, to discover if any money was concealed therein. Suspecting there was more money in the house, they then brought Mr. Lawrance down again, and threatened to cut his throat; and Fielder put a knife to it, as if he intended to do it; to make him confess what money was in the house. One of them took a chopping bill and threaten'd to cut off his leg: they then broke his head with their pistols, and dragged him about by the hair of his head. Another of them took the kettle of water off the fire, and flung it upon him; but it did no other harm than wetting him, because the maid had just before taken out the greatest part of the boiling water, and filled it again, with cold. After this they dragged him about again, swearing they would "do for him" if he did not immediately inform them where the rest of his money was hid. They then proceeded to make a farther search; and in one of the rooms, they found a chest which belonged to Mr. Lawrence's son, of which they turned out 20l., with some odd matters of plate and bed-linen, and then withdrew; threatening to return again in half an hour, and kill every one they found loose. So sayings they locked them all in the parlour, and took the keys of the back and front door, and threw them down the privy, which was in the area.

Turpin by this robbery got but little, for out of the 26l. they took in the whole, he distributed it among them all but three guineas and six shillings and six pence.

A proclamation was issued for the apprehension of the offenders, and a pardon and 50l. was offered to any of the party who would impeach his accomplices, which, however, had no effect. The White Hart, in Drury-lane, was their place of rendezvous. Here they planned their nightly visits, and here they

Turpin and Fielder's Cruelty to Mr. Lawrance, to make Him discover his Money.

divided their spoil, and spent the property they had acquired.

The robbery being stated to the officers of Westminster, Turpin set off to Alton, where he met with an odd encounter, which got him the best companion he ever had, as he often declared. King, the highwayman, as he was returning from this place to London, being well dressed and mounted, Turpin seeing him have the appearance of a substantial gentleman, rode up to him, and thinking him a fair mark, bid him stand and deliver, and therewith producing his *pistols*, King fell a laughing at him, and said " what dog rob dog! Come, come, brother Turpin, if you don't know me, I know you, and should be glad of your company." After a mutual communication of circumstances to each other, they agreed to keep company, and dievide good or ill fortune, as the trumps might turn up. In fact King was true to him to the last, which was for more than three years.

They met with various fortunes; but being too well known to remain long in one place, and as no house that knew them would

Turpin and King, robbing Mr. Bradele, on the Loughton Road

receive them in it, they formed the resolution of making themselves a cave, covered with bavins and earth, and for that purpose pitched upon a convenient place, enclosed with a thicket, situated on the Waltham side of Epping, (a place large enough to receive them and their horses;) near the sign of the King's Oak. And while they lay quite concealed, they could through several holes, discover the passengers as they went along the road; and as they thought proper, would issue out and rob them.

In this place Turpin lived, ate, drank, and lay, for the space of six years, during the first three of which he was enlivened by the drollery of his companion, Tom King, who was a fellow of infinite humour in telling stories, and of unshaken resolution in attack or defence.

One day, as they were spying from their cave, they discovered a gentleman riding by, that King knew very well to be a rich merchant near Gresham College. The gentleman was in his chariot, and his wife with him; his name was Bradele. King first attacked him on the Laughton road; but he being a man of great spirit, offered to make resistance, thinking there had been but one; upon which King called Turpin, and bid him hold the horses heads. They proceeded first to take his money, which he readily parted with, but demurred a good while upon parting with his watch, which he said was a family piece, being the dying bequest of his father. King was insisting to take away, when Turpin interposed, and said, they were more of gentlemen than to deprive any one of their friend's respect which they wore abou them, and bid King upon this desist from his demand. This souccession on the part of the robbers induced the gentleman to ask a further favour, which was that they would permit him to purchace his watch back again? Upon which King said to Turpin, " Dick, he seems to be a good honest fellow, shall we let him have the watch?" " Aye," said Turpin, " do just as you will. " Bradele inquiring what would be the price, King said six guineas, adding, we never sell one for more, if it be worth six-and-thirty; upon which Mr. Bradele said he would leave the money at the Sword-blade Coffee-house in Birching-Lane; when Turpin cried out, Aye, but King, insist upon no questions being asked.

On the day after this transaction they went to the Red-Lion alehouse, in Aldersgate Street, where, they had not been more than an hour, when Turpin heard of the approach of the chief constable and his party: they mounted each their horse; but before King could get fairly seated he was seized by one of the party, and called on Dick to fire. Turpin replied, " If I do, I shall hit you." " Fire, if you are my friend," said King— Turpin fired, but the ill-fated ball took fatal effect in King's breast. Dick stood a moment in grief, but self-preservation made him urge his mare forward to elude his pursuers; it was now he resolved on a journey to York, and raising himself in his saddle, he said, " By G—, I will do it." He now struck into Shoot-up-hill Lane, West End, Hamstead Heath, crossed the hill, the Hendon Road, Crachshall Common, and the road to Highgate, in sight of his pursuers. Coming to a high gate in a narrow path to the right, his mare carried him gaily over it, while his pursuers lost time in opening it. He now passed on to Hornsey and Duval-lane, where a crowd endeavouring to intercept him; he presented a pistol in each hand, and bore down all before him. Old Hornsey toll-bar had then a "chevaux de frieze" in the upper rail, and the toll-keeper hearing the cry of " Stop him," had shut the gate, but Dick patting his mare's neck, she cleared the whole, to the astonishment of every one. He then struck into a bye lane, through Tottenham and Edmonton, and coming up to a man with a donkey cart, who not being able to get out of his way, stood in the middle of the road. An encouraging word to Bess made her clear the driver and his little cart, while the astonished crowd saluted him with " Hark away Dick."

He now passed along Enfield Highway, and coolly lighted his pipe, relying on the bottom of his steed that he could not be overtaken. He stopped at a public house near Ware, and gave his mare a draught of ale, and had a tankard himself; for which he gave the landlord aguinea. It now became dark, but he continued his solitary course, and at the end of fifty miles, Bess did not appear to have turned a hair in her fine skin. He now enters Huntingdon, asses the bridge over the Ouse, and as he passed through Huntingdon, the clock struck eleven, having rode sixty miles in four hours! Having come up to the York stage, he was recognized by a passenger, and when he had held his hat above his head, as saluting the person, the guard fired a shot through the hat, thinking it was on his head. Turpin whipping the horses on one side darted by them like lightning. On he rode till he passed Northampton County, and stopped at a small public-house, called the Burleigh Arms, where the ostler-lad knew him as a good customer; here he ordered the astonished lad to bring him three bottles of brandy, a pail of water and a good beef steak. The first was brought, " But there was no fire to cook by," said the lad. " Never mind that," said Dick, " cut off a good slice raw." Dick then well scraped and dried his mare, and washed her all over with brandy and water, and then rolled the raw beef round the bit of the bridle. He had just got into the saddle again, when he heard his pursuers approaching him; he could not go out the front way, but the lad showed him a back, which led to a great declivity, over which they would not venture to follow him: this he slid down in safety, and resumed his rapid career. His mare being revived by the spirits imbibed through the skin, and the raw beef-steak, seemed to fly as on wings. They now passed Grantham, and moved rather slowly up Gonorby Hill. His attention was now drawn to a gibbet near to the road, on which hung the skeletons of two malefactors. He now drew aside to look, and reflect a little : on approaching it, he was surprised by the sudden appearance of an aged female, with wild haggart look. After a little conversation he learned that the two skeletons were those of her two sons, and that she had been deserted by her gang, and come here determined to die in the vicinity of her deceased sons. This was the old gypsy Barbara, to whom he was well known in her better days. This may be my fate was his reflection; and bidding her good-night, he passed onwards to Newark, the Trent, the Wade of Sherwood, and is now once more on Yorkshire ground, full 150 miles from London! Bawtry Thorne, and Selby, are now passed: on passing the deep Don, he was grieved to see that Bess appeared distressed. His fingers being numbed, he bridle down, and Bess stumbled and fell, but started up immediately, giving Dick a look that said, "I am not hurt." He now gave her a bottle of liquor, which so reinvigorated her, that she neighed aloud. After taking a drop from his brandy bottle, he mounted as quickly as his stiffened limbs would enable him. By evening he was on the road to Cawood, and the Duse soon appeared before him. Between 5 and 6 o'clock he reached the ferry of Cawood, but his galled steed was nearly exhausted. He hailed the ferryman on the opposite side, and the boatman had scarcely reached the middle of the stream, when he again heard the shouts of his pursuers, who had changed horses above twenty times, in order to come up with, and take him. No time to be lost, he quietly walked down to the river side, and Bess plunged into it with her rider, whom she bore to the other side in sight of his pursuers. Refreshed by her cold bath, she soon regained the road, but it was the last effort m of a noble-hearted anal. Encouraged by "Harkaway Bess," she flew on. The pinnacles of York appear. "It is won," exclaimed Dick. Astonishing to relate, he reached York the same evening, and was noticed playing at bowls in the bowling-green with several gentlemen there, which circumstance saved him from the hands of justice for that time. His pursuers coming up and seeing Turpin, knew him; and caused him to be taken into custody: one of them swore to him and the horse he rode on, which was the identical one he arrived upon in that city; but on being in the stable, and its rider at play, and all in the space of four-and-twenty hours, his *alibi* was admitted; for the magistrates at York could not believe it possible for one horse to cover the ground, being upwards of 190, miles, in so short a space. It was a race that equalled, if not surpassed, the first achievements of turf velocity.

For the two last years of his life he seems to have confined his residence to the county of York, where he appears to be a little known. He often accompanied the neighbouring gentlemen in their parties of hunting and shooting; and one evening, on a return from an expedition of the latter kind, he saw one of his landlord's cocks in the street, which he shot at and killed. One Hall his neighbour seeing him shoot the cock, said to him, Mr. Palmer, you have done wrong in shooting your landlord's cock; where-

Turpin taking a Flying Leap, over the Donkey Cart

upon Palmer said if he would stay whilst be charged his piece he would him too. Mr. Hall hearing him say so, went and told the landlord what Palmer had done and said. Thereupon the landlord immediately went with Mr. Hall, to Mr. Crowle, and got his warrant for apprehending him; by virtue of which warrant he was next day taken up, and was committed to the house of correction, at Beverly.

The next day Mr. Hall received a letter from Rodert Appleton, Long-Sutton, with this account:—that the said John Palmer had lived there about three quarters of a year, and had before that been once apprehended, and made his escape, and that they had a strong suspicion he was guilty of horse-stealing.

Another information gave notice, that he had stolen a horse from Captain Dawson, of Ferrarby; his horse was that which Turpin, *alias* Palmer rode on when ne came to Beverly, and which he had stole from off Hickington Fen in Lincolnshire.

The following is a letter, he wrote to his brother in Essex.'

Dear Brother,   *York, Feb, 1739.*

I am sorry to inform you, that I am now under confinement in York Castle, for horse-stealing. If I could procure an evidence from London to give me a character, that would go a great way towards my good, and might procure in the end my enlargement and acquittal. It is true I have been here a long while, but never wrote before. Few people know me. For Heaven's sake, dear brother, do not neglect me: you will know what I mean when I say,   *I am yours,*   *John Palmer.*

His brother refused to take the letter, and it was returned unopened to the post office in Essex, because the brother would not pay for it.

He wrote to his father upon being convicted, to use his interest to get him off for transportation; but his fate was at hand; his notoriety caused application to be ineffectual. To his letter the father returned the following answer:

Dear Child,

I received your letter this instant with a great deal of grief. According to your request, I have writ to your brother John, and Madam Peck, to make what intercession can be made to Colonel Watson, in order to obtain transportation for your misfortune; which had I 100l. I would freely part with to do you good. In the mean time my prayers are for you; and for God's sake give your whole mind to beg of God forgiveness for your transgressions. The Lord be your comfort and receive you into his everlasting kingdom.   *I am your distressed,*

Hempstead,   *Your loving father,*
March 29th, 1739.   *JOHN TURPIN.*

After he had been in prison five months, he was removed from Beverly to York Castle to take his trial. When he was on his trial, his case seemed much to effect the hearers. He had two trials, upon both of which he was convicted upon the fullest evidence. After a long trial, the Jury brought in their Verdict, and found him *Guilty*.

He was carried in a cart to the place of execution, on Saturday, April 7th, 1739. He behaved himself with amazing assurance, and bowed to the spectators as he passed. It was remarkable that as he mounted the ladder, his right leg trembled, on which he stamped it down with an air, and with undaunted courage looked round about him; and after speaking near half an hour to the topsman, threw himself off the ladder, and expired in about five minutes.

R le & Co., Printers, 2 & 3, Monmouth court, 7 Dials.

THE COW.

This animal is something like the bull in respect to size and nature, of which she is the female; but of all quadrupeds, she seems most liable to alteration from the quality of her pasture; and this is more observable in other countries than in our own. Thus, Africa is remarkable for the largest and the smallest cattle of this kind, as are also Poland, Switzerland, and several other parts of Europe. Among the Eluth Tartars, where the pastures are remarkably nourishing and luxuriant, the cow becomes so large that few men can reach the tip of its shoulders; but in France, where the animal is stinted in its food, and driven from the richest pasturage, it greatly degenerates.

The cow has seldom more than one calf at a time, and goes about nine months. Her nature and use being so well known, we decline a further description.

The zebu, or Barbary cow, is more like the bison than the cow, having a lump on its shoulders, which weighs from twenty to forty pounds. They are frequently saddled like horses, and are likewise used in drawing chariots, carts, &c. Instead of a bit, a ring or small cord is passed through the cartilage of the nostrils, which is tied to a larger cord, and serves as a bridle.

EASY LESSONS.

Thou, O Lord, hast maintained my right and my cause; thou sittest on the throne and judgest rightly.

Thou hast rebuked the heathen and destroyed the ungodly; thou hast put out their name for ever and ever.

The Lord also will be a defence to the oppressed; even a refuge in the time of trouble.

The rich and the poor meet together. The Lord is the Maker of them all.

A prudent man foreseeth the evil, and hideth himself; but the simple pass on, and are punished.

He that oppresseth the poor to increase his riches, and he that giveth to the rich, shall surely come to want.

Be not amongst wine-bibbers; amongst riotous eaters of flesh.